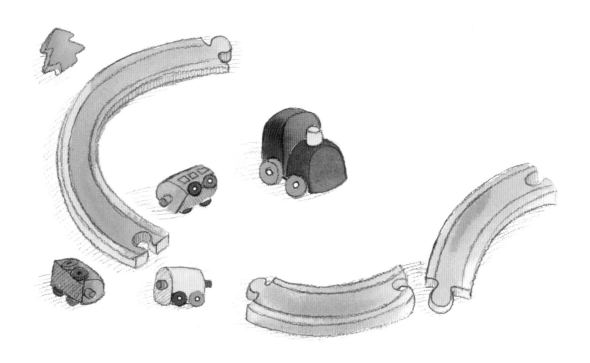

This edition published by Parragon Books Ltd in 2016 and distributed by

Parragon Inc.
440 Park Avenue South, 13th Floor
New York, NY 10016
www.parragon.com

Written by David Beford   Illustrated by Susie Poole

ISBN 978-1-4748-5740-6

Printed in China

You're a **BIG** Brother

Bath · New York · Cologne · Melbourne · Delhi
Hong Kong · Shenzhen · Singapore

You're going to be a big brother!
Hurray! How lucky are you?

Babies LOVE their big brothers

and all the smart things that they do.

Babies are funny and friendly,

but there are things a big brother
soon knows ...

Babies can SMELL ...

and pull hair as well ...

so watch out and hold onto your nose!

Babies make moms and dads busy—
they won't just be caring for you.

But now that you're a big brother,
it's fun sharing with somebody new.

Babies don't do much to start with,

so just quietly show them your toys.

They can't dance or sing,

but they like
to join in ...

by making a gurgling noise!

Babies learn lots from big brothers,
so teach them all you can do:

Share and
take care ...

be baby's best friend,

and they'll be amazing ...

just like YOU!